The Little Rippers

Volume 1:
Here Come the Little Rippers!

By: Rebecca Munsterer

Novel Nibble Publishing
Norwich, Vermont

Novel Nibble Publishing, August 2013
Copyright @ 2013 by Rebecca Munsterer

Published in the United States by Novel Nibble, Vermont
August 2013

Illustrations by Ryan Hueston

Printed by CreateSpace, An Amazon.com Company

"When out of the forest,
They came one by one.
Their skis pointed downward.
Their limits seemed none.

Tiny in stature,
But strong as the wind.
They appeared like fresh snowflakes,
No one knew where they'd been.

Brash as the eagles,
And swifter than owls.
Theirs was the ski slope,
To share amongst pals.

I watched from afar.
There was no room for fibbers.
For young ones live fearless.
They are *Little Rippers*."

-Winchell Windspeed

For Gus Gentine, who rips it up.

Table of Contents

Chapter 1:
Away We Go

Max hadn't eaten a pancake in almost a month. This was surprising, considering that pancakes were Max's favorite food. If given a choice between chocolate-chip ice cream or pancakes, he would pick pancakes. Max had a pancake passion.

But for the past thirty days, Max had only eaten scrambled eggs for breakfast. By giving up pancakes before his annual trip to Vermont, he knew that he would appreciate Grandpa's famous "lumberjack pancakes" even more.

"Can you drive any faster, Dad?" Max asked his father from the backseat of the family's car. "I can't wait to see Grandpa."

"Relax," Max's older sister, Molly, said as she put down her *Girl Time* magazine. "We just passed the Welcome to Vermont sign. It won't be much longer."

For one weekend every January, brother and sister, Max and Molly Beckett, visited their Grandpa at his home in Vermont. It was their favorite weekend of the year because Grandpa lived right next to Powderhound Mountain, their favorite ski resort.

"Now, don't forget kids," Mrs. Beckett said from the passenger seat, "be careful when you're skiing Powderhound. Wear your helmets."

"We always wear our helmets, Mom," Molly rolled her eyes.

"And don't go too fast," Dad added.

"But going fast is the point of skiing!" Max exclaimed.

"The point of skiing is spending time outdoors with your sister," replied Mr. Beckett.

"I'd rather spend time outdoors by myself," Molly said as she crinkled her nose at her younger brother and went back to reading her magazine.

After another hour of driving on Vermont twisty back roads, the Beckett family turned left on Long John Lane. The car bumped and bounced on the dirt road as Max held tightly to his seatbelt. He recognized Grandpa's house immediately when he saw the infamous crooked window on the second floor.

As Mr. Beckett parked the car in the driveway, the front door of the house opened. "Well, it's about time," Grandpa hollered through his whiskers as he stepped out on the porch. "My lumberjack pancakes were starting to get cold."

"Lumberjack pancakes?" Molly asked as she opened the car door and stepped out on the snow-covered ground. "But it is nearly eight o'clock at night!"

Grandpa smiled. "Well, someone told me that Max has been waiting a whole month for pancakes with real Vermont maple syrup. I figured breakfast for dinner could be fun."

"Yessss!" Max squealed, as he ran toward the house. He stopped in his tracks a few feet away from his grandfather. "Grandpa! What happened?"

Grandpa patted a brace on his right leg. "Oh, this thing? I had to get my knee fixed. It's no big deal."

Mr. Beckett stepped out of the car and walked over to Grandpa. "Why didn't you tell us?"

Grandpa laughed. "Because you would have worried about me. I'm perfectly fine. I'll be back on skis in a few weeks."

"A few weeks?" Mrs. Beckett asked as she carried two suitcases away from the car. "But who is going to ski with the kids?"

"Don't worry. I've got it all figured out. Give me the kids' suitcases, and get on your way. You two should have a lovely anniversary weekend in Montreal." Grandpa escorted Mr. and Mrs. Beckett back to their car. "Now, get going!"

Mr. Beckett waved from his seat as he backed the car out of the driveway. "Be good, kids. See you on Sunday!"

"Bye Mom! Bye Dad!" The kids waved.

"Don't worry about a thing!" Grandpa yelled.

After their parents left, Max and Molly raced to Grandpa's kitchen. Max always loved Grandpa's kitchen because it was filled with interesting things. Copper pots hung from hooks near the stove. A pile of shiny red apples balanced in a cherry wood bowl. A collection of vintage glass bottles stood like soldiers on the windowpane above the sink. But most importantly, a piping-hot, sky-high pile of lumberjack pancakes sat on the kitchen table.

"Oh boy!" Max said as he ran to the table and picked up a fork.

Molly joined him and placed a napkin on her lap. "I still think it's weird to have pancakes for *dinner*... but I'm definitely not complaining."

"Hold up," Grandpa interrupted as he entered the kitchen and took a seat between the kids. "Before we start our meal, there is something I have to tell you."

"Is something wrong, Grandpa?" Molly asked. "Are we not skiing this year because of your knee?"

"Well, I will not be skiing this year. But both of you will be. Since I can't ski with you... I signed you up for a kids ski group."

"A kids ski group?" Molly asked. "But the kids up here are dorks. They don't even know who Jackson Blade is."

"I don't know who Jackson Blade is," Grandpa chuckled.

"He's only the dreamiest pop star of all time," Molly sighed as she twirled a piece of her long, curly hair.

"I want to ski with you, Grandpa," Max chimed in. "I don't want to ski with strangers."

"But they won't be strangers once they become your friends," Grandpa smiled. "And you kids are now old enough to ski with friends. Why, Max, you're in third grade! And, Molly, you're in fourth grade!"

"Fourth grade is half-way over. So, technically, I'm in fourth and a half grade," Molly quipped.

"Well that means that I'm in third and a half grade. But, that doesn't mean that I won't miss you, Grandpa," Max said.

Grandpa smirked at his grandson. "I'll be back out there next year, kids. But this year, you'll have a fun adventure with new friends. Now, dig into those lumberjack pancakes. They won't stay warm very long."

After a fun-filled night of pancakes and board games, Max and Molly snuggled into their respective bunk beds in Grandpa's den. They had slept in the same bunk beds for years... Max in the top bunk and Molly in the bottom bunk. After

Grandpa turned out the light and wished them goodnight, Max tossed and turned.

"Molly," Max whispered. "Molly, wake up."

"Go to sleep, Max," Molly whispered back. "Grandpa's waking us up at six o'clock in the morning."

"I know, but I'm really nervous about tomorrow. We only ski once a year. What if the other kids don't like us? What if we can't keep up?"

"Well, if that happens we'll just stay in the lodge and drink hot chocolate. Now, go to sleep! Staying up worrying isn't going to make you a better skier tomorrow."

"I guess," Max grumbled as he pulled his sheets over his head. He shut his eyes, and tried to dream about pancakes.

Chapter 2:
Tiger Print Ski Pants

The next morning, after buying lift tickets at the main lodge, Grandpa dropped off Max and Molly at the Kids Activity Center.

"Do you want me to wait here with you?" Grandpa asked.

Molly shook her head no, while Max simultaneously nodded his head yes.

Grandpa laughed at his grandchildren. "Well, in that case, I'll just go find myself a seat in the lodge right around the corner. I'll be there all day if you need me."

Max held on to his Grandpa's leg. "You might want to order me a hot chocolate since I might be there sooner than you think."

"Stop being such a baby," Molly whispered to her brother. "The other kids are looking at you."

Grandpa leaned over and looked Max in the eyes. "You'll be fine, kiddo. You're here to have fun. Now, go put your ski boots on. They'll be calling you into groups soon."

As Grandpa left, Max and Molly took a seat at a nearby table. The Kids Activity Center was filled with children of all ages… from young snowboarders wearing droopy pants to older skiers wearing bright patterned jackets. Every kid was wearing a helmet, and nearly all of them had season passes hanging around their necks. (Max and Molly felt like outsiders for having their day lift tickets sticking out from their coat zippers.)

After Max and Molly changed into their ski boots and stored their backpacks in a nearby cubicle, a woman with two long braids and a blueberry-colored jacket stepped to the front of the group. She carried a clipboard filled with paper. "Welcome to the Powderhound Kids Activity Center. My name is Heidi, and I'm the head of the program. In a moment, I'll assign groups for the weekend. But before we begin, please raise your hand if you have participated in a Kids Activity Group once before at Powderhound."

Nearly all of the kids raised their hands. Max and Molly just looked down at their boots.

"Great! It looks like nearly all of you are familiar with our program. Now, let's split up into groups!" She flipped through papers on her clipboard. "Elliot Banks, you're in the Shredding Shorties. Katie Washburn, you're in the Mogul Maniacs. Anna Wu, you're in the Tucking Tikes. Chase Chittenden, you're in the Little Rippers."

Each kid walked over to a different section of the activities center.

Heidi continued to read. "Molly Beckett, you're in the Little Rippers."

Molly picked up her helmet and goggles from the table and walked over to her group.

"Max Beckett, you're in the Carving Kiddos."

"No!" Max blurted. "I mean, I would rather be in the Little Rippers, please."

Molly's cheeks turned bright pink. "Max!" she exclaimed, unimpressed that her brother desperately wanted to be in her group.

Heidi just nodded her head and smiled. "Okay then, Max. You can be with your sister in the Little Rippers. We'll just swap out another kid for the Carving Kiddos."

"Thank you," Max replied as he zipped up his old green jacket and quickly walked over to Molly.

"Try not to embarrass me," Molly whispered as she furrowed her brow at her brother.

After reading the rest of the kids' names off the list, Heidi smiled at the five groups. "All right kids, you're now in your permanent groups for the weekend. I'll ski with the Little Rippers, and the four other team leaders will each take another group. Tomorrow, each group will nominate one racer to compete in our weekly Sunday Funday Race."

"Sunday Funday?" Max whispered to Molly. "That sounds exciting."

"Don't get your hopes up," Molly explained. "I'm sure that neither of us will be nominated. They probably only let the really good skiers race."

Heidi continued with her speech. "Our number one goal is to have fun in the great outdoors. Now, let's go outside and ski."

Max and Molly followed Heidi outside to the ski slope. They picked up their skis from the rack where Grandpa had left them, and circled up with the other Little Rippers. As they clicked their boots into the bindings, Max and Molly eyed up the other kids. There were two other boys and one other girl, all of whom were a bit taller than Max, but a little shorter than Molly. They were all wearing flashy colors, like hot pink and electric blue. One of the kids was even wearing tiger-print pants.

As the group made their introductions, Max and Molly listened closely.

Chase Chittenden was the kid wearing tiger-print ski pants. He was a fifth grader who lived with his parents in Powderhound Village. Since he was a local, he skied with a kids group every weekend. Molly noticed that he had fancy *curved* race poles, so she knew that he would be fast. Plus, he had been nominated to be the Sunday Funday racer every week for the past month.

Jenna Duke was a third grader who lived with her mom in Colorado. Her dad lived in Vermont, and she was currently visiting him for the week. She had MANY ski resort stickers on her pink helmet. She had even had a sticker from a ski area in *Switzerland.*

Wyatt Evans was a fourth grader who lived in Florida but was on vacation with his family for the weekend. He was a Junior Olympic water-skier who was looking to rip up the slopes like he ripped up the lakes. He looked really athletic and strong.

When it was time for Molly and Max to introduce themselves, they didn't have much to say.

"I'm Molly. I like the color purple and playing soccer. I'm from Pennsylvania, and I don't get the chance to ski very often."

"You can tell she doesn't ski often," Chase laughed. "Her goggles are on upside down."

The other kids giggled. Molly flipped around her goggles, ashamed of her silly mistake.

Max was next to introduce himself.

"And I'm Max, Molly's little brother. I'm in the third grade, and I learned how to ski black diamonds last year with my Grandpa."

"Black diamonds are for babies," Chase teased. "We ski *double* black diamonds around here."

"Now, Chase," Heidi clarified, "we ski all sorts of terrain. And we all start out on warm-up runs. C'mon, let's get on the lift."

Heidi and Jenna boarded the high speed quad first. Behind them, Molly and Max lined up with Chase and Wyatt for the next lift. But, when Molly and Max moved forward to board, Chase pulled Wyatt back by the jacket. "We don't want to go on with those kids. Let's wait and go on by ourselves."

Molly and Max were swiftly taken away by the quad. Max sighed as he pulled down the safety bar. "I have a feeling Chase doesn't like us."

"Obviously, Max," Molly whined. "Did you see his poles? He's a real racer who skis double black diamonds. He's probably afraid we're going to hold him back."

"Hey Pennsylvania people," Chase yelled from the chairlift behind. "Turn around."

Molly and Max turned around as a snowball flew towards their chair. The snowball missed Max's helmet by only a few inches. "I really miss Grandpa," Max said, unhappy.

At the top of the hill, the Little Rippers re-grouped.

"Okay, kids, let's take a nice easy run down Cat Track Trail. Make big turns, keep your eyes on the slope, and smile while you ski. We'll meet back at the chair lift."

Max and Molly started skiing down the hill with the group. Jenna made a lot of fast, short, slalom turns, while Wyatt made long, meandering, wide turns.

Max, desperately concentrating on the slope, fell over a mogul. His poles and skis flew through the air. "Phooey," he said as he shook snow from his body.

Molly stopped and picked up his poles. As Molly carried the poles to Max, Chase skied by and purposefully checked his skis to the side. A huge spray of snow hit Max and Molly in the face.

"If you fall… you get snowballed," he cackled as he skied away.

"I'm not sure skiing with the Little Rippers was a good idea," Molly said.

Chapter 3:
Following the Leader

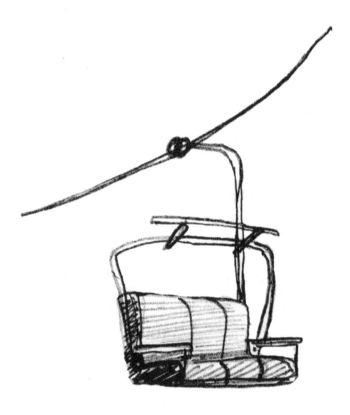

After a second chairlift ride, Molly and Max circled up with Heidi and the other Little Rippers.

"Kids, on this run we're going to play follow the leader," Heidi announced. "Whatever you do, make sure you stay in a line. I'll go first. Then Max, then Chase, then Molly, then Wyatt, and finally Jenna."

The Little Rippers lined up behind Heidi. As they skied, Chase started to pass Max. Max tried really hard to go fast, but Chase dropped into a tuck and gained ground. "See ya later, snail face," Chase sneered as he flew by.

When Heidi stopped halfway down the slope, Chase had already made his way to the front of the line. "Chase, you are supposed to stay behind the person in front of you," Heidi instructed. "If you don't follow the rules, you won't be able to play our games."

"But what if the person in front of me was slower than a three toed sloth?"

Max angrily squinted through his goggles at Chase.

"Then, you aren't making enough turns," Heidi insisted. "Let's try it again on the next run, and this time, no funny business."

On the following run, the Little Rippers lined up in order and started to ski behind

Heidi. This time, Max was able to stay ahead of Chase. Max pushed with his poles, and huffed and puffed as he skied as fast as possible.

As the Little Rippers skied down the trail, it started to snow. At first, small, graceful snowflakes swirled around the winter sky. However, in mere moments, the snowflakes grew larger and fell faster. Max had a hard time seeing Heidi through the blinding blizzard. In fact, his goggles eventually became completely covered with snowflakes. Max couldn't see *anything*. He had to stop.

The other Little Rippers stopped behind him. "Wow," said Jenna. "I've never seen it snow this hard. Where's Heidi?"

"I don't know," Max said as he wiped snow from his goggles with his mitten. "I couldn't see which way she went."

The Little Rippers stood at the crossroads of two trails. The trail signs were impossible to read, as they too were covered with snow.

"Chase," Molly said, "you know this mountain well. Which way should we go?"

"I'm not sure," Chase shrugged. "Usually, we go to the double black diamond side," he furrowed his brow at Max, "not the babyish green circle side."

"Both trails probably end up at the same place," Jenna said. "In Colorado, there are a million trails, but most of them end up near the main lodge."

Molly leaned in and looked at her brother. "Are you *one-hundred percent* sure that you don't know which way Heidi went?"

"I'm sure," Max admitted. "But, if I had to make a guess, I would say that she went to the left. Or maybe the right. No, the left." He thought hard for a moment. "Yep, definitely the left."

"Well then, what are we waiting for?" Wyatt asked as he started to ski. The Little Rippers followed, one by one, skiing close together since they could barely see the slope.

After what seemed like a mile, the Little Rippers finally reached the bottom of the run. "This doesn't look familiar," Wyatt announced.

In fact, there was nothing familiar about the landscape. There was no chairlift. No lodge. No Heidi. No…nothing. In fact, it wasn't much more than a flat area of snow-covered land.

"I'm scared," Jenna admitted. "Where are we?"

Chase shook his head. "I'm not sure. And as someone who grew up on this mountain, it takes a lot to get me lost."

"This is my fault," Max shook his head.

"You bet it's your fault, snail face," Chase growled. "You should have been able to keep up with Heidi."

Molly knew that her brother could sometimes be a pain. But she also knew that Chase was not being fair. "Blaming Max isn't going to help anything," Molly said. "This isn't his fault. Now, everyone take off your skis. We better start hiking back up to the top."

"Hiking?" Chase laughed. "That will take us all night."

"Do you have a better idea?" Molly asked as she leaned over Chase. She was sick of his attitude. Being a pessimist was bad enough. But being a pessimist in a blizzard was even worse.

Chase cowered under Molly's stare. "You're the boss," he said as he popped his boots out of his bindings.

The rest of the Little Rippers followed suit and started hiking up the mountain. Hiking was difficult, as the kids' ski boots submerged under the new snow with every step. The blizzard continued to whirl around the kids while they slowly tried to gain altitude.

Suddenly, a voice echoed from the forest. "What are you kids doing on my property?"

Chapter 4:
Trespassing

The Little Rippers could barely see each other in the blizzard. So, they certainly couldn't see the man approaching on a snowmobile. But, they could *hear* him.

The voice was deep and stern. "I said... why are you kids trespassing on my property?"

The Little Rippers focused their eyes on a blurry object in the distance. In the middle of the snowstorm, a man wearing a red and black flannel shirt appeared on a snowmobile.

"Trespassing?" Max asked. "Mister, we don't mean to trespass. We just followed the ski trail down here, and this is where we landed."

"Shush Max," Molly scorned. "We're not supposed to talk to strangers."

"Well you better talk to someone," the stranger laughed. "You five kids aren't going to survive out here in this blizzard. Where are your parents?"

"Back at Powderhound Mountain, sir," Jenna said.

"Well, you kids just skied down a private ski trail. Didn't you read the sign?"

"No, sir," Wyatt responded. "The trail signs were covered by snow."

"You should have kept a trail map in your pocket! I could report you to the police for trespassing."

"Please don't get us in trouble," Jenna spoke up. "We really didn't mean it."

The stranger inspected the group of kids. He looked them up and down, examining their faces and their ski equipment. "How do you kids think you're going to get back to Powderhound?"

"We're going to hike, sir," Molly said.

"Hike?" the stranger laughed. "In this blizzard, you'll freeze like popsicles." He looked at Max, who was already shivering. "I guess I'll have to take you back, but I only have room for one of you on the snowmobile at a time. Which one of you wants to go first?"

Jenna, Chase, Wyatt and Max all raised their hands.

"No!" Molly yelled. "We're not splitting up. We're the Little Rippers and we're together in this mess. We're not leaving unless we all leave together."

The stranger nodded in agreement. "You're a smart girl, young lady." He scratched his head. "So, we need to figure out a way to get you all out of here together."

The stranger and the Little Rippers all thought to themselves for a moment.

"Hey!" Wyatt piped up. "Do you have a rope?"

The stranger reached into his snowmobile storage compartment and pulled out a rope. "Actually, I do. I use it to tie off my property lines from trespassers like you."

Wyatt grabbed the rope and inspected it carefully. "This should work. We can tie it to the back of the snowmobile. All five of us can hold on to the rope and ski back up the mountain. It will be just like waterskiing behind a boat."

"I don't know, Wyatt," Jenna said. "It sounds really difficult."

Wyatt shook his head. "It's not difficult at all. Trust me. It will be fun."

Wyatt and the stranger tied the rope to the back of the snowmobile. The kids held tight to the rope, lining up with the girls on the right side of the rope, and the boys on the left.

The stranger took his seat on the snowmobile and counted down. "Three... two... one...hold on, Little Rippers!"

The snowmobile took off slowly to allow the Little Rippers to gain their balance. Eventually, it accelerated faster in order to get up the steep slope. The Little Rippers clenched tightly to the rope, as snow sprayed up from the underside of the snowmobile. As they climbed the mountain, they swerved and bounced on the wild ride.

Finally, the snowmobile reached the summit. The Little Rippers released the rope, as Wyatt hooted with joy. "Wah-hoo! That was awesome!"

The stranger turned off his snowmobile and untied the rope. "Good job, kids," he smiled. Then, his grin turned to a scowl. "Now go back to where you came from, so I can go back to my own business."

"Wait a minute," Molly hesitated. "There is no trail. Where did you take us?"

Chapter 5:
Trees, Schmees

The Little Rippers looked around the mountain. There were no trails in sight. There were no skiers either. It was a beautiful landscape, but it certainly didn't seem to be part of the ski area.

"Where are we?" Molly asked the stranger on the snowmobile.

The stranger smiled. "This is the secret back bowl of the mountain. Nobody is allowed to ski here…with the exception of me." He looked out at the landscape. The snowstorm had started to clear, and there was a beautiful view of a ragged mountain peppered with green evergreen trees.

"Why didn't you take us back to the front side of Powderhound where we started?" Jenna asked.

"Because if I took you back there, people would have seen me. I don't want anyone to see me."

"But why?" Jenna continued to ask.

"Because I said so," the stranger said forcefully before turning the key of his snowmobile. The engine hummed.

"Well, what are we supposed to do?" Molly yelled. "Are you just going to leave us here?"

"You kids are Little Rippers, right? Then you should know how to ski trees. Just head straight down this slope, and you'll eventually pop out on the woods near the lodge."

"I've never skied trees before," Max admitted.

The stranger squinted at Max, confused. "You've never skied trees?"

Max shook his head. "Never. But I'll be fine if I go slowly. I'm the slowest in the group anyway."

The stranger raised his eyebrow. "You love skiing, kid?" the stranger asked.

Max nodded his head. "Even though I'm the slowest in the group, I enjoy skiing the most."

"Well, let me tell you a little secret about going fast," the stranger whispered. He reached into his pocket and gave Max a small bar of gold-colored ski wax. "Here's a little something to sprinkle on the bottom of your skis tonight. Tomorrow, you'll be skiing past the others."

"Thanks," Max said as he examined the bar. "But what kind of wax…"

"Now get out of my woods," the stranger interrupted. "Go! All of you!"

The Little Rippers started skiing down to the edge of the woods as the stranger pulled away on his snowmobile. As he disappeared, Max noticed him privately crack a smile. Eventually, the stranger was gone, and the Little Rippers were on their own.

"These look like pretty easy birch tree glades," Jenna announced to Max. "If you keep your eyes on the space between the trees and not the trees themselves, you should be fine. It's a trick I learned in the back bowls of Wyoming."

"You really have skied everywhere, haven't you?" Wyatt asked.

"I've never skied the back bowls of Powderhound until now. Here we go!" Jenna smiled as she pushed off her poles and skied down the mountain.

The Little Rippers followed, taking their time to ski safely. Molly made wide sweeping turns around the birches. Chase jumped over a stump. Wyatt ducked under a branch. And Max hooted and hollered as he tried to avoid tree trunks.

"Whooooooooaaa!" Max wailed.

"Trees, schmees!" Chase howled.

"Kowabunga!" Molly screeched.

"Yeee-haaawww!" Wyatt roared.

"Holey macaroni!" Jenna screamed.

Finally, the Little Rippers could see a trail through the trees. "That's it!" Molly yelled to the others with glee. "That's the bunny slope at Powderhound. We've found our way back to the mountain."

"Bombs away," Chase yelled as he tucked toward the trail. He hit a mogul coming out of the woods and landed on the bunny slope with a thump.

The other Little Rippers eventually all popped out of the trees. They congregated together on the side of the trail as they gave each high fives.

"Max, those woods were definitely a double black diamond! Congratulations, little guy. Skiing doesn't get any harder or steeper than that!" Wyatt smiled.

"Yay," Max cheered. "That was awesome."

"Awesome?" a voice from up the trail echoed. A man in a red and white jacket skied toward the kids. It was the Ski Patrol. "I don't think it is awesome to cause an area-wide emergency search." He pulled a radio out of his pocket and spoke into the speaker. "This is the Ski Patrol calling Heidi. I've found the five missing kids."

"I have a feeling that we're in a lot of trouble," Molly sighed.

Chapter 6:
Punished

Heidi paced back and forth in front of the Kids Activity Center at the base of the mountain. When she saw the Little Rippers appear with the patrolman, she ran to them.

"Where have you been?" she asked the kids.

"On a little adventure," Jenna responded as she smiled sheepishly.

Heidi counted the Little Rippers one by one. "Molly. Chase. Jenna. Wyatt… and Max." Heidi fell to her knees and gave the kids a group hug. "Are you all okay?"

"We're better than okay," Chase said.

"Well, that's great news," Heidi breathed a sigh of relief. "But you are all in deep trouble. What happened?"

"It's a long story," Molly began. "It all started when Max couldn't see where you went in the blizzard."

"And then we took a wrong turn," Max continued.

"And we skied down to nothing," Jenna said.

"And a man let us ski behind his snowmobile," Wyatt interrupted.

"And he made us ski the trees," Chase smiled.

"And, well, we ended up landing on the bunny slope," Molly finished. "It was pretty cool."

"Whoa, kids…slow down," Heidi said, confused. "Who was the man on a snowmobile?"

All of the Little Rippers shrugged.

"And where exactly did he drop you off on the mountain?"
The Little Rippers shrugged again.

"He said it was a secret back bowl," Jenna explained.

Heidi looked suspiciously at the Little Rippers. "This story is hard to believe. I've skied the front, back, and side of this mountain, and I've never seen any secret back bowls."

"We're not lying, Heidi. This story is the truth," Molly insisted.

"Well, you kids had me incredibly worried. It's very dangerous to go off on your own. The entire Ski Patrol has been looking for you all day."

"We're sorry, Heidi," the kids all said together.

"Well, as a punishment, the Little Rippers won't be able to participate in the Sunday Funday race tomorrow."

"Bah-humboogers," Chase complained. "I was going to win that race."

"Instead," Heidi continued, "all five of you will work as gatekeepers for the race."

"That means we can't ski at all!" Jenna exclaimed. "We have to stand around all day on the race trail!"

"That's correct. Now, you all need to get to the main lodge. Your family members are waiting for you. And they'll be happy to know that you're all okay."

When Max and Molly arrived in the lodge, Grandpa ran to them. "You kids had me scared to death. I'm too old for this type of scare. I almost had to call your parents in Montreal."

"I'm so sorry, Grandpa. This was all a mistake," Molly hugged her grandfather.

"Grandpa, we never meant to worry you!" Max cried.

"Well, let's get you both back to my house. It's been a long day for all of us."

That night, Max pushed spaghetti around on his plate. He usually loved a hearty pasta dinner after a day of skiing. But that evening, he couldn't even stomach a meatball.

Grandpa couldn't help but notice Max playing with his food. "What's wrong, sugarplum?"

"It's the Little Rippers. They hate me," Max blurted out.

"Fiddlesticks! Why would they hate you?" Grandpa asked.

"Because I ruined everything. I took the wrong turn today, and now none of the Little Rippers can race tomorrow."

"Don't blame yourself, Max," Molly chimed in. "We all got lost together."

Grandpa smiled at his grandson. "Max, my boy, you can't change the past. The best thing you can do is learn from your mistakes in the future. The Little Rippers don't hate you. In fact, even though you've all been punished, you still might be able to have fun tomorrow."

"I guess," Max agreed. "But it stinks to not ski. I really wanted to try my new ski wax."

"What ski wax?" Grandpa asked.

Max ran to Grandpa's moose-antler coat rank. He reached in the pocket of his old green jacket and pulled out a bar of wax. "This ski wax."

"Let me see that," Grandpa insisted as he held out his hand. Max handed over the bar, and Grandpa inspected it. The wax was gold-colored, and perfectly smooth. It glittered in the light of the overhead table lamp. "Goody gumdrops! Gold wax! Who gave this to you?"

"The man on the snowmobile. He said to rub it on my skis. Apparently, it will help me keep up with the faster kids."

"He was pretty grumpy," Molly added, "but we wouldn't have found our way out of the forest without him."

"Did he tell you his name?"

Molly and Max shook their heads.

Grandpa held the bar of gold wax up to the light. He looked at his grandkids in awe. "Well, I know who the stranger is."

Chapter 7:
An Old Hermit

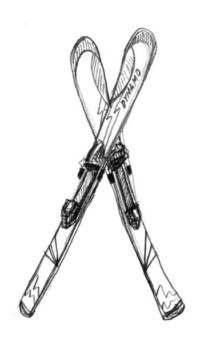

The next morning, Max and Molly rejoined
Heidi and the other Little Rippers at the bottom of

the chairlift. Grandpa accompanied them, in order to set the record straight.

"I'm afraid that the kids were not lying about their adventure yesterday," Grandpa said to Heidi.

"How do you know?" Heidi asked.

Grandpa reached into his coat pocket and pulled out the bar of gold-colored wax. He handed it to Heidi.

Heidi inspected the glitzy wax. "Holy moly! Is that what I think it is? Winchell's Wax?"

"Winchell?" Chase asked. "As in Winchell Windspeed? The Olympic legend?"

"That's correct, young man," Grandpa confirmed. "Winchell Windspeed, the best American downhill skier in recent history. This is his famous homemade wax. Nobody knows what's in it, but Winchell used to make it for his own skis."

Heidi looked at the Little Rippers. "Winchell was the first person to ever ski from the summit of Powderhound Mountain straight down to the base lodge in under a minute. He's a legend… but he's also a hermit." She looked at Grandpa. "Nobody has seen him in over ten years."

"Well, these kids saw him yesterday," Grandpa confirmed. "And I believe their entire story." Grandpa put his arms behind Molly and Max.

"I thought I recognized that guy," Jenna reflected. "Now, I remember his face from my Dad's old ski posters."

"Winchell was very famous years ago," Heidi said. "But he thought that people were getting too wrapped up in the money behind ski racing. He wanted people to love the sport, not the money. So, he disappeared from the limelight and was never seen again. Some people thought he moved to the islands where he would be far away from the ski slope. But, I always thought his heart would keep him in the mountains."

"You kids met a legend yesterday," Grandpa nodded.

"And to think that Molly told Max not to talk to him since he was a stranger," Wyatt announced.

"Did you really say that?" Grandpa asked his granddaughter.

Molly nodded.

"She also told us to stick together," Max bragged. "My big sis is a real smarty-pants."

"I'm so proud of you," Grandpa patted Molly on the shoulder. "You're really a trustworthy young lady."

"Does this mean we're still in trouble?" Chase asked, hopeful.

"Well," Heidi began, "you may have been telling the truth, but you still got lost and caused a lot of worry." She scratched her head. "On the other hand, you did stay together as a group, and showed good judgment. I think we might just be able to enter the Sunday Funday race today after all."

"Hooray!" The kids cheered.

"Now, we better hurry up," Heidi looked at her watch. "The race starts in a few minutes and we need a racer. Who should we nominate?"

"Chase is certainly our strongest skier," Wyatt said.

"And he has the Dynamo Double Turbo skis! They are the fastest skis you can buy," Jenna chimed in.

"But there's one thing I don't have," Chase admitted. "Winchell's wax."

Max took the golden wax from Heidi's hand, and handed it to Chase. To Max's surprise, Chase refused it.

"No, Max," Chase said. "This wax was given to you, and you're the person who should use it."

"But, I'm not as fast as you," Max admitted.

"It doesn't matter who is the fastest on the slopes, it only matters who is the smartest in the course. And you're going to ski smart!" Chase looked over at Heidi. "I nominate Max to be our racer."

"Me too!" Wyatt agreed.

"And me!" Jenna added.

"Go, go, little bro!" Molly laughed.

"Well then, I guess it is unanimous," Heidi announced. "Max is our Little Ripper racer for the day. Now, let's get that wax melted on his skis and we'll be ready to go."

"Already done," Grandpa smiled. "I had a feeling Max would be racing today, so I woke up early and waxed his skis." Grandpa leaned toward his grandson and whispered in his ear, "Go get 'em kiddo."

Max smiled up at his grandfather. "Thanks, Grandpa!"

"Let's go, Rippers," Heidi cheered. "Get your boots and skis on, and we'll meet at the top of the course."

Chapter 8:
Broomsticks and Puddles

The Sunday Funday race was actually a minute-long obstacle-course. It was set on a trail directly under the chairlift so that the public could watch the event. The other teams were already inspecting the course by the time the Little Rippers arrived at the start gate.

"You're going to do great!" Molly proclaimed to Max.

"I hope so, Molly," Max said. "These skis feel awfully fast though." He slid his skis back and forth on the snow. "I'm not sure I can handle the speed."

"Okay, kids, let's snowplow through the course," Heidi announced. "Remember, the idea here is to stick together and help Max plan his attack."

The Rippers slid around the start gate and down to the first obstacle. The first "gate" was a horizontal broomstick. The racers would have to duck under the broomstick in order to make the gate.

"Perfect!" Max smiled. "I'll just limbo under the stick. I have lots of limbo experience from birthday parties."

Chase shook his head. "You'll want to be in a tuck, not a limbo. If you lean forward, you'll be faster since your weight will be downhill."

"Got it," Max nodded. "You're the expert!"

The next obstacle was a puddle skim. A large, shallow, puddle of water had formed between two gates.

Wyatt inspected the puddle. "As someone who knows a lot about water skiing, you definitely do *not* want to get stuck in that water." He skied over to a lip on the slope near the puddle. "You'll want to use this bump to launch you OVER the puddle. You'll be much faster in the air, and you'll land right after the water."

Heidi nodded her head in agreement. "Smart thinking, Wyatt!"

The third obstacle was a series of mammoth-sized moguls. Max was nervous, since he had never skied moguls of that size.

Jenna stepped up to the coaching challenge. "I ski a lot of moguls in Colorado. And I know from experience that it is faster to zip around the ruts than to thump over the top. Try to stay in the tracks around the bumps, and you'll be speedy."

"Sounds good, Jenna," Max said. "I'll try."

The last obstacle was also the most intimidating. The final gate was set next to a powerful snowblower. Each racer would have to ski through forceful blows of snow as he or she entered the finish line.

"What if the snow covers up my goggles?" Max asked Heidi. "I won't be able to see the finish."

Molly skied over to her brother. "Max, remember last summer when we set up the water sprinkler in the backyard?"

Max nodded, as he looked at his sister questionably.

"I stole the hose and chased you around the backyard. I sprayed you while you tried to catch me. You couldn't see anything but you quickly caught me since you followed my voice."

A smile appeared on his face. "That was actually pretty fun. You really soaked me, but I pushed you in the pool later that day."

"Well, I'll be at the finish line cheering you on," Molly announced. "You can just ski in the direction of my voice. You'll hear me, just like you did in the backyard with the hose."

"Sounds like a plan, sis!" Max smiled. "Now, let's get up to the start. I don't want to miss the race!"

By start time, spectators had lined the race trail. Some carried cow bells to cling and clang for the racers. Some carried cameras to take pictures. Even others held signs, cheering on their favorite skier.

At the top of the course, the other racers stretched and warmed up for their runs. They were all wearing skin-tight race suits and fancy new equipment. Max felt embarrassed by his old green jacket and hand-me-down skis.

Molly could tell that Max was intimidated.

"Don't worry about the other kids. Just believe in yourself," Molly said.

"And believe in the wax," Chase laughed.

Max and the Little Rippers watched the first racer take out of the start. Trevor Hartley, from the Mogul Maniacs, was really fast but he fell on the first gate. He skied right into the broomstick, and slid down the hill on his back. It made Max even more nervous.

Heidi sensed Max's nerves. "If you fall, just get up and ski to the side of the course. Simply participating in this race makes you a winner."

The race starter called a few other names. Elliot from the Shredding Shorties. David from the Tucking Tikes. Ginny from the Carving Kiddos. Finally, it was time for Max's run. "Max Beckett, next in the gate."

"I'll see you at the bottom," Molly said as she started to ski away. "Remember to listen for my voice at the finish line. I'll meet you there."

Max skied to the starting hut. Heidi, Chase, Jenna, and Wyatt stood outside the hut, cheering loudly together for Max:

> *Little Rippers*
>
> *Little Rippers*
>
> *We don't fall 'cuz*
>
> *We're not trippers!*

Max took a deep breath as he slid into the start. He double checked his pole straps. He re-fastened his helmet buckle. And most importantly, he tightened his goggles.

"Max Beckett in the gate," the starter announced. "Racer ready. Three-two-one... go!"

Max pushed as hard as he could out of the start, just like those Olympic racers he had seen on television. As he headed for the first obstacle, the broomstick, he dropped into a tuck and went quickly underneath. The Little Rippers cheered loudly.

Next, Max made his way to the puddle. He took a quick left before the puddle and hit the bump Wyatt had pointed out during inspection. The crowd all gasped while Max flew through the air. He landed on the far side of the puddle as the spectators cheered.

The moguls were next. Max remembered to stay in the ruts. He pretended like the moguls were trees from his previous day's adventure. He kept his eyes on the tracks between the moguls, and ignored the moguls themselves. He zipped right around the bumps in record time. Spectators rang their cowbells in celebration of his speed.

Finally, Max approached the last obstacle, the snow blower. The snow blew powerfully on Max, as he tried to push his way through the man-made blizzard. He listened intently for Molly's voice, but the sound of the snowblower was incredibly loud. Even though Molly was screaming at the top of her lungs at the finish line, Max simply couldn't hear her.

The Little Rippers gasped from the side of the course as he disappeared into a cloud of white snow.

"MAX!" Molly shrieked.

Seconds went by with no sign of Max.

"He can do it," Heidi whispered to herself. "I just know he can."

Finally, a snow-covered blob emerged on the course. It was Max. He was blanketed in snow from helmet to boot, but he moved very swiftly towards the finish line. When he crossed, his time was announced on a nearby speaker.

"Max Beckett from the Little Rippers. One minute and two seconds. Our first place finisher."

Grandpa was the first to give Max a hug in the finish area. Molly was second. The rest of the Little Rippers skied to the bottom of the course as Max wiped the snow from his body.

"You did it, Max!" Chase roared. "I always knew you could do it!"

Max rolled his eyes as he shook Chase's hand. "I have a feeling that when you sprayed snow on me yesterday morning you didn't think I could win a race."

"I was just preparing you for the snow blower," Chase grinned.

All of the other Little Rippers jumped up and down in celebration of Max's big finish.

"Congratulations, Max," Heidi said. "And as the fastest finisher, you won a new pair of Dynamo *Triple* Turbo Skis." Heidi handed Max a pair of shiny brand-new race skis.

"Wow!" Chase admired. "Those are next year's model. You can't even buy them in stores yet."

Max looked down at his old skis. They looked pretty shabby compared to the Dynamo Triple Turbos. But, they were sentimental. "You know, I think I'll keep the ones I have. Maybe you can give the Dynamos to someone who really needs them."

Grandpa smiled over at his grandson. "I think that's a very nice thing to do."

"If you say so," Heidi agreed. "I'm sure I can find someone who can't afford a new pair of skis. This might help them learn to love the sport."

As Max's competitors approached him for a congratulatory handshake, someone in a flannel jacket and a ski mask cut the line.

"Great job out there, young man," the man said.

"Thanks," Max responded as he looked the man in the eyes. Even with the ski mask, Max knew in an instant it who it was.

Chapter 9:
One Last Run

Max knew that the stranger in the ski mask was Winchell Windspeed. Max smiled from ear to ear as he talked to the famous Olympian. "Winchell, I couldn't have done it without your famous gold…"

"Shh…" Winchell whispered. "Keep your voice down, kid. I've got to run, but I just wanted to say congratulations."

As Winchell started to ski away into the crowd, Max followed him. "Hey," Max said as he pulled on his flannel jacket. "Do you want to take a quick run with us? The chairlift runs for a few more minutes."

Winchell looked around and thought for a second. "Sure," he nodded slowly.

Max yelled over to Heidi and the other Little Rippers. "Hey guys! Let's take one last run!"

Heidi looked over at the stranger in the ski mask. Then, she looked at the Little Rippers knowingly. "C'mon, kids. I think there's time for one final run of the day."

Winchell, Heidi and the Little Rippers caught the last chair of the day at Powderhound Mountain. They skied fast down the hill, giggling and chasing each other on skis. Winchell was a really good skier. Max tried to keep up with him, but even with his newly waxed skis, Winchell was just too speedy.

At the end of the run, Winchell smiled from ear to ear. "I haven't had this much fun in years. Skiing with you kids reminds me of the good ol' days."

"Maybe we can ski with you again another time?" Molly asked.

"You're always invited to join us," Heidi added.

Winchell nodded. "I have a feeling I'll see you again on the slopes. But for now, I have some work to do back home. It seems that I need to re-wax my skis to make sure that none of the Little Rippers ever catch up with me!" He laughed and patted Max on the helmet. "Have fun at the after party, kids."

"Have fun skiing, Winchell!" Max smiled.

The Little Rippers all waved goodbye to their new friend. Within seconds, Winchell skied to the bunny slope and disappeared into the woods.

For the rest of the afternoon, the Little Rippers continued their celebration. They ate maple syrup sugar snow. They had a friendly snowball fight against the Carving Kiddos. And, most importantly, they spent time enjoying each other's company.

As the sun set on Powderhound Mountain, the Little Rippers prepared for the end of their ski weekend. They returned back to the Kids Activity Center to pack up their bags.

"Thanks for everything, Heidi," Molly said.

"You bet, kids!" Heidi smiled. "You are all invited back to the Little Rippers group anytime."

Chase, Jenna, and Wyatt all lined up to hug Max and Molly goodbye. They vowed to ski together the following year during the same January weekend.

"And don't forget to practice your tree-skiing," Max smiled at his new friend, Chase. "I wouldn't want to beat you down the slope, snail face," he joked as he gave Chase a high five.

An hour later, Mr. and Mrs. Beckett picked up their kids at Grandpa's house. They had enjoyed their weekend in Montreal, but admitted that they missed Max and Molly's company. "How was the weekend, kids?" Mrs. Beckett asked upon their return.

Molly smiled silently while Max winked at his grandfather. "The best weekend ever!" Max exclaimed.

"We had a great time with Grandpa," Molly added. "He's the best."

"You kids are the best," Grandpa grinned. "And, you're invited to visit anytime. The snow doesn't melt on the mountain until April. Perhaps you can visit again before the end of the season!"

"You bet!" Max smiled. "I want to get back up here as soon as possible."

After kissing Grandpa goodbye, the Becketts returned to the road. Pennsylvania was many hours away on the highway, and Max and Molly were sure to fall asleep on the long drive.

After snuggling into his car seat, Max watched the Vermont landscape change outside his window as his family drove south. Max was incredibly tired, but also incredibly thankful for the weekend with his new friends. He couldn't wait to tell his schoolmates in Pennsylvania about the Little Rippers. And most importantly, he couldn't wait to plan his next ski trip.

The End

Acknowledgements

Thirty years ago, my Dad put a rope around my waist and sent me skiing ahead of him on Chicken Delight at Hidden Valley, New Jersey. Eventually, I lost the rope. But I never lost my love for skiing with my father.

Last winter, Dad and I were skiing the slopes of Sugarbush, Vermont on a bluebird day. While we were waiting for the lift, I noticed that we were surrounded by kids. They were flashy. They were fast. And their skis were unrecognizable from the straight skis I learned on years ago. But their passion for the sport was recognizable.

At that moment, a light bulb went off. As a writer, I had always loved writing kids' stories. But what if I could wrote a story for *ski* kids? I decided to give it a try.

The Little Rippers is a family effort. I'd like to thank my sister (who still is faster than me in gates, even though I hate to admit it) for being my editor. I'd like to thank my mom for being the number one fan of the Little Rippers facebook page. I'd like to thank Jamal, for helping me figure out the "business behind the book." I'd like to thank Jon, for inspiring my ski-crazed characters. I'd like to thank Ben and Gus Gentine for being real Little Rippers.

And of course, I'd like to thank Ryan Hueston, who has created the beautiful Little Ripper images.

But most of all, I'd like to thank my Dad. He'll always be the ultimate Big Ripper. And although I'll never catch him, it's always fun to try.

Grandpa's
Lumberjack Pancakes

(Adapted recipe from the kitchen of Barbara Simmons)

Lumberjack pancakes are the perfect start to the day for the Little Rippers! Ask your parents for help when cooking in the kitchen.

Ingredients

(Makes Six Large Pancakes)

2 eggs
2 tablespoons sugar
1 cup blueberry yogurt
2 tablespoons melted butter
1 and 1/2 cups flour
1 teaspoon salt
1 and 1/2 teaspoons baking soda
1/2 cup milk
1/3 cup chocolate chips
1 banana, sliced
Maple syrup
Powdered sugar

1. Beat the eggs and sugar together. Slowly add the yogurt and melted butter.
2. Sift the flour, salt and baking soda together, then add into the egg mixture.

3. Thin with enough milk to adjust the batter to the consistency of heavy cream. (You may not need all of the milk).
4. Fold in the chocolate chips and bananas.
5. Drop spoonfuls of the batter onto a hot griddle. Flip when bubbles appear on the surface of the pancakes. Let the other side brown.
6. Serve warm to your favorite Little Ripper friends with maple syrup and powdered sugar. Enjoy!

Little Rippers Ski Activities

Wherever the Little Rippers ski, they like to have fun! Here are some of their favorite activities on and off the slopes!

1. **Molly's Memory Game for Chairlift Rides**:

Molly knows that the chairlift can sometimes be long and cold. So, she likes to play games to pass the time! Here's one of her favorite games:

Start with the sentence, "I'm going to the lodge and I'm going to eat…" and then add a food object of your choice. (In Molly's case, she would add a slice of cheese pizza.) Then, the next person must repeat everything that was already said, plus one new item. For example, "I'm going to the lodge and I'm going to eat a slice of cheese pizza, and a bowl of chicken noodle soup." Keep going, until someone can't remember ALL of the items. Then, start from the beginning!

2. **Max's Safety Habits**

Max knows that it's important to practice ski safety. Here are some tips for always being prepared on the slopes:

Make sure to always follow the rules of the ski area. Feel free to introduce yourself to a Ski Patroller, and always ski with a partner. Carry a trail map, and familiarize yourself with the area. It also can't hurt to carry a treat in your pocket (for snacking on the chairlift) and an emergency contact name. (Max keeps Grandpa's phone number in his pocket.) Have fun, be safe, and enjoy hot cocoa at the end of a great day!

3. Jenna's Do-It-Yourself Ski Placemats

Jenna loves to make homemade gifts… especially if they have to do with skiing. Here's Jenna's favorite do-it-yourself gift idea!

Pick up a few trail maps at your favorite ski area. Ask your parents for help laminating both sides of the trail maps at home with clear contact paper. (Contact paper sticks to the maps, making them shiny and waterproof.) Ta-da! Give these placemats as gifts to ski friends!

4. Chase's Recipe for Maple Sugar Snow

As a Vermonter, Chase really loves Vermont Maple Syrup. He regularly treats himself to a special sweet treat. Try it with your family!

With permission from your parents, drizzle a few teaspoons of Maple Syrup on freshly fallen snow. (Watch out for dirty snow. No yellow snow, please!) Immediately, take a spoon and scoop up the sugary snow. Enjoy!

5. Wyatt's Physical Challenge

Wyatt knows that regular exercise is an important part of being prepared for the ski season. In addition to skiing, here are some great ways to get fresh air during the winter:

> A. Making snow angels on freshly fallen snow
> B. Figure skating or playing pond ice hockey
> C. Shoveling your neighbor's porch
> D. Sledding in your backyard
> E. Building the tallest snowman on your street

Made in the USA
Middletown, DE
28 February 2022

61926704R00046